This book belongs to:

....

....

Quarto is the authority on a wide range of topics.

Quarto educates, entertains and enriches the lives of our readers—enthusiasts and lovers of hands-on living.

www.quartoknows.com

Author: Saviour Pirotta
Illustrator: Olivia Beckman
Designer: Victoria Kimonidou
Editor: Ellie Brough

This edition first published in 2018 by QED Publishing,
an imprint of The Quarto Group.
The Old Brewery, 6 Blundell Street,
London N7 9BH, United Kingdom.
T (0)20 7700 6700 F (0)20 7700 8066
www.QuartoKnows.com

A catalogue record for this book is available from the British Library.

ISBN 978 1 91241 330 0

Manufactured in Guangdong, China TT052018

9 8 7 6 5 4 3 2 1

Little Red Riding Hood

Written by Saviour Pirotta
Illustrated by Olivia Beckman

Once there was a girl
who had a lovely red coat,
with a red hood.

People called her **Little Red Riding Hood.**

One day her mother put some cakes in a basket. "Granny's ill," she said. "Why don't you go and see her?"

So Little Red Riding Hood
set off with the cakes.

"Stay on the path and
don't talk to strangers!"
warned her mother.

Little Red Riding Hood reached the woods and saw some beautiful flowers. She wandered off the path to pick some for her granny.

As soon as she left the
path, she met a wolf.

"What's in your basket?"
he asked sweetly.

"Cakes for my granny," answered
Little Red Riding Hood.

"Where does your granny live?" the wolf asked.

"Further along the path," replied Little Red Riding Hood. "In a little cottage."

While Little Red Riding Hood picked some flowers, the wolf hurried along the path.

When Little Red Riding Hood arrived
at Granny's cottage, she called out:

"Granny, it's me."

"Come in.
The door's open,"
wheezed Granny.

She was tucked up in bed,
with the curtains closed.

"Granny, what **big ears** you have!"
said Little Red Riding Hood.

"All the better to hear you with, my dear," Granny whispered.

"Granny, what **big eyes** you have!" said Little Red Riding Hood.

"All the better to see you with, my dear," said Granny.

"Granny, what **big teeth**
you have!" said Little Red Riding Hood.

"All the better to
EAT you with!"
snarled Granny,
leaping out of bed.

"Help!" Little Red Riding Hood cried.

It wasn't Granny at all. It was the big, bad wolf and he wanted to gobble her up!

The horrible wolf chased her
round and round the cottage.

"Help! Help!"

Little Red Riding Hood shouted.

Luckily, a woodcutter heard her calling and ran to see what all the noise was about.

The woodcutter saw the wolf and raised his axe.
The wolf took one look and jumped out of the window.

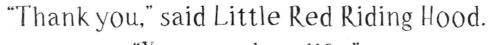

"Thank you," said Little Red Riding Hood.
"You saved my life."

"You must never, ever talk to
wolves," said the woodcutter.
"What is that knocking?"

Little Red Riding Hood rushed over to open the wardrobe where the knocking was coming from. She found Granny, safe and well. The wolf had shut her inside.

"Goodness! Thank you," Granny said to Little
Red Riding Hood and gave her a big hug.

Little Red Riding Hood put
the kettle on and they all had
cake and a nice cup of cocoa.

And Little Red Riding Hood never strayed
off the path in the woods again.

Next Steps

Discussion and comprehension

Ask the children the following questions and discuss their answers:
- Why was Little Red Riding Hood taking cakes to her Granny?
- Why did Little Red Riding Hood's mother warn her not to talk to strangers?
- Look at the pictures in this book, which of the characters do you like the best?
- Who was the hero in this story? Can you say why?

Learn about adjectives

Ask the children to think about the wolf. What kind of character is he? Is he good or bad? Show the children where the author describes the wolf as 'horrible'. Explain that words we use to describe are called adjectives. Ask the children to give you a description of the wolf using at least three adjectives. Make a list of the adjectives given and ask the children to write their description of the wolf using at least three of the adjectives.

Create a card

Give the children a range of coloured paper, card, tissue paper, coloured pens, glue and scissors. Ask them to make a get well card for Little Red Riding Hood's Granny. Explain that the card should have flowers on the front and a nice message inside.